Disney
EATS

MORE THAN

20 RECIPES FOR EVERYDAY
COOKING AND
INSPIRED FUN

JOY HOWARD

Disney
EDITIONS

Los Angeles • New York

Alien
TOAST for TWO

PREP
10 min

COOK
10 min

SERVES
2

Our take on avocado toast is sure to prompt an "ooooooooooh" from any **TOY STORY FAN**. Pair it with sliced fruit for a satisfying meal.

INGREDIENTS

½ **small avocado**

Kosher salt

Black pepper

2 slices whole wheat bread

1 tablespoon cream cheese

6 black olives

6 baby spinach leaves

DIRECTIONS

1 In a small bowl, use a fork to mash the avocado until smooth with a few small bits. Season with salt and pepper and stir well. Set aside.

2 Toast the bread slices. Place each slice on a plate, then spoon and spread half the avocado onto each piece as shown.

3 Divide the cream cheese into six portions. Roll each into a ball, flatten it slightly, and arrange three dots on each slice of toast for the eyes. Trim the hatched end from each olive and press one on each dot of cream cheese.

4 Use kitchen shears to trim four of the spinach leaves into ears, and tuck two in place on each slice of toast beneath the avocado. Trim an antenna and mouth from each of the remaining leaves and arrange as shown. Serve immediately.

Helpful
TIP

Keep the avocado from browning before you eat by adding a squeeze of lemon or lime juice. The citric acid in the juice helps slow down the oxidation process that causes discoloration.

Bacon & Egg
MOUSE-WICH

What's better than a **GRAB-AND-GO** breakfast sandwich from a fast-food joint? One you make at home that begins with a **FROM-SCRATCH** biscuit! We've topped this version with the usual fixings but added a handful of **SPINACH** to each sandwich for a boost of green goodness.

INGREDIENTS

6 slices bacon

2 cups flour

4 teaspoons baking powder

1 teaspoon kosher salt

½ cup plus 8 teaspoons margarine

1 cup whole milk

8 teaspoons olive oil

4 large eggs

4 slices cheddar

1 cup baby spinach

Special equipment
Mickey Mouse silicone breakfast mold

DIRECTIONS

1. Heat the oven to 400°F and line a baking sheet with foil. Arrange the bacon in a single layer on the sheet and bake until crisp, about 15 minutes. Transfer to a paper towel-lined plate and set aside.

2. In a large bowl, stir together the flour, baking powder, and salt. Use two knives or a pastry cutter to cut in ½ cup margarine. Blend in the milk until combined.

3. In a cast iron skillet over medium-low heat, melt 2 teaspoons margarine. Center the silicone mold in the skillet and fill with batter. Cook the biscuit covered until browned underneath, about 4 minutes. Remove the mold (carefully, as it will be hot), flip the biscuit, and cook covered until brown on the other side, about 4 minutes more. Continue with the remaining batter and margarine. Halve each biscuit lengthwise.

4. Wipe the skillet clean and warm 2 teaspoons olive oil over medium heat. Crack an egg into the skillet and cook until the whites are set and the center is still slightly runny, about 3 minutes. Slide the egg onto a biscuit half and top with a slice of cheese. Repeat with the remaining eggs, biscuits, and cheese. (If you like, the assembled sandwich halves can be kept warm in a 200°F oven while you make the rest of the eggs.)

5. Halve each slice of bacon and add three pieces to each sandwich. Top off each with ¼ cup spinach and the other biscuit half. Serve immediately.

Fit for a *Princess* SMOOTHIE BOWLS

UNLEASH YOUR INNER ARTIST and update your Instagram feed by assembling one of these healthy BREAKFAST bowls—each inspired by a different Disney PRINCESS.

Moana's SUNSHINE BOWL ↗

blend:

¼ cup shredded coconut + 1 frozen banana
+ ¼ cup frozen cantaloupe + ½ cup Greek yogurt
+ 2 mandarin oranges

top with:

sliced almonds + shredded coconut
+ blueberries + mandarin orange slices
+ green grapes

Ariel's
DEEP BLUEBERRY SEA BOWL

blend:
1 frozen banana + **½ cup frozen blueberries**
+ **¼ cup Greek yogurt**
+ **splash of milk**

top with:
sliced kiwi + **star fruit** + **strawberries**

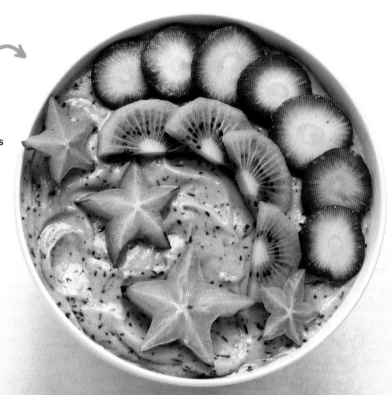

Snow White's
BEWITCHING APPLE BOWL

blend:
⅓ cup apple juice + **1 frozen banana**
+ **1 cup frozen mango** + **4 ice cubes**

top with:
sliced strawberries and blueberries
+ **half an apple**

Eeyore PANCAKE STACK

PREP
5 min

COOK
25 min

MAKES
1 serving

Though the most sullen resident of the Hundred-Acre Wood is **FAMOUSLY** not much of a morning creature, there are few cuter ways to **CAPTURE** him than in an Eeyore pancake breakfast. Using a **SQUEEZE** bottle for the batter will make shaping his face and ears far simpler than using a spoon. If you don't have a squeeze bottle on hand, put the batter in a plastic bag, snip a corner, and **PIPE AWAY**.

INGREDIENTS

1 cup of your favorite pancake batter

Cooking spray

Chocolate sauce, for garnish

Plain Greek yogurt, for garnish

4 blueberries

Special equipment
Food-grade squeeze bottle

DIRECTIONS

1 Place the batter in the squeeze bottle. Warm a nonstick skillet over medium heat. Coat with cooking spray, then use some of the batter to pipe a rounded diamond-shaped ear in the pan. Cook until bubbly and golden on the underside, about 4 minutes. Flip and continue to cook until golden, about 2 minutes more. Transfer to a plate and repeat, cooking another diamond-shaped ear and an oval for Eeyore's face.

2 To assemble, pipe a bit of chocolate sauce near the edge of a plate for Eeyore's hair, as shown. Set the oval pancake in place just below, then layer the ears on top. Use the yogurt and blueberries to add a pair of eyes and a muzzle, as shown. Finish by piping on more chocolate hair, eyebrows, and a line of chocolate stitching down the center of Eeyore's face. Serve immediately.

King of All
VEGGIE PLATTERS

PREP
10 min

COOK
10 min

SERVES
2

Please growing stomachs—and **SIMBA FANS**—with a **REGAL SPREAD** featuring healthy veggies and dip. Strips of bell pepper make **SIMBA'S WAVY MANE**, but if you're not a fan you can achieve a similar look with baby carrots.

INGREDIENTS

1 (8-inch) whole wheat tortilla

1 red radish

¼ cup of your favorite hummus

½ red bell pepper, ribs and seeds removed

2 pitted black olives

DIRECTIONS

1 Use a 3-inch round cookie cutter to shape two circles from the tortilla. With kitchen shears, snip one round in half to form Simba's mouth, then trim the other round to form the bridge of Simba's nose, as shown.

2 Cut two 1½-inch rounds from the remaining tortilla for the ears. Halve the radish and slice two thin rounds from one portion for the eyes. Trim the remaining half in the shape of a nose.

3 Spread the hummus in a circle in the center of a plate. Place the tortilla nose and mouth, and radish eyes and nose, as shown. Cut the pepper into curved strips and arrange around the hummus. Add the tortilla ears and finish with sliced olive pupils and olive strip eyebrows.

Helpful TIP

You can't make this ferociously cute platter in advance, but you can get ahead on the prep. Cut the pepper strips for the mane, then wrap them in a wet paper towel and seal in a ziplock bag. The peppers will stay crisp for at least two days.

Hidden Mickey
APPLE SLICE SANDWICHES

It's not hard to spot the **FAMOUS** pair of ears on this fruit snack that's perfect for a late-afternoon nosh. What's more, you don't need any **SPECIAL TOOLS** to create Mickey's shape—a mini round pastry cutter and a small round pastry tip (or drinking straw) will do.

INGREDIENTS

1 large apple

⅓ cup of your favorite nut butter

¼ cup crisp rice cereal or chopped almonds

DIRECTIONS

1 Cut the apple crosswise into ¼-inch-thick slices (you should have enough for 4 sandwiches). Remove the seeds. To form Mickey's head, use a mini round pastry cutter to cut a circle in the center of half the slices. Cut two small ears atop each head with the end of a round pastry tip.

2 Spread the remaining apple slices with a heaping tablespoon of nut butter so that it reaches the edges. Press a cut slice on top of each.

3 Place the rice cereal in a small bowl. Dip the edges of each sandwich in the cereal to coat the nut butter.

Helpful TIP

Add a nutritional boost to this snack by using brown rice cereal in place of conventional rice cereal.

Baymax COCOA

The **HERO** that inspired this cozy recipe is cleverly made with **PILLOWY** marshmallows. We like the look (and taste) of melted **CHOCOLATE** for his face, but you can save some time by drawing it on with a **BLACK FOOD WRITER**.

INGREDIENTS

2 regular marshmallows

6 mini marshmallows

¼ cup chocolate chips

4 tablespoons unsweetened cocoa powder

4 tablespoons sugar

Pinch of salt

2 cups of your favorite milk

BAYMAX HOW-TO ⤵

DIRECTIONS

1 With kitchen shears, snip a slit on two sides of each regular marshmallow to form Baymax's arms, as shown. For the legs, snip a small piece from the end of 4 mini marshmallows. Attach a pair to each body by using the sticky end of each along with a dab of water.

2 Snip a small piece from the end of the two remaining mini marshmallows and use the sticky side and a dab of water to adhere it to the top of each body.

3 Melt the chocolate according to the package directions. Use a toothpick to apply chocolate eyes to each head, as shown. Set aside.

4 In a small saucepan over medium-low heat, whisk together the cocoa, sugar, salt, and 2 tablespoons milk. Warm until the cocoa and sugar are dissolved, then add the remaining milk and heat, whisking occasionally, until hot.

5 Evenly divide the cocoa between two mugs. Garnish each with a marshmallow Baymax and serve immediately.

Night Howler
LEMONADE

PREP
5 min

COOK
3 hr 15 min
(includes freezing time)

SERVES
4

A dash of **UNEXPECTED COLOR**—inspired by the havoc-wreaking flower featured in *Zootopia*—can lend a **DRAMATIC** touch to a classic summer drink. Blend each glass with an equal amount of your favorite IPA for a simple and **REFRESHING** cocktail.

INGREDIENTS

4 cups of your favorite prepared lemonade (a light-colored drink works best), chilled

Blue food coloring

Lemon slices, for garnish

Special equipment
Star-shaped ice or food mold

DIRECTIONS

1 Fill the mold with water and freeze until solid, about 3 hours.

2 In a large pitcher, stir together the lemonade with 2 drops food coloring. If needed, add another drop or two to reach the desired hue.

3 Evenly divide the drink into glasses and add a few star ice cubes. Garnish with lemon slices and serve.

Bambi
BENTO

PREP
5 min

COOK
10 min

SERVES
1

We'll admit that throwing together a plain turkey sandwich is **SIMPLER** than making what's featured in this recipe. But it wouldn't be anything to **FAWN** over. Pulling off this sweet-looking **WOODLAND** meal requires just a few extra minutes, and it is **EASIER** to assemble than you might think!

INGREDIENTS

2 slices whole wheat bread

Mayonnaise or mustard, for spreading

2 slices deli turkey

1 slice your favorite cheese

3 blueberries

2 slices honeydew melon, cut ½-inch thick

2 tablespoons ranch dressing

¼ cup black olives

¼ cup bunny-shaped crackers

Special equipment

Butterfly-shaped cookie cutter

DIRECTIONS

1 With a sharp knife, cut the bread slices into the shape of Bambi's head, as shown (they should be identical). Reserve a 2-inch piece of crust. Spread one side of each bread slice with mayonnaise or mustard. Trim a slice of turkey and the cheese to fit in the bread, then sandwich them between the slices. Use a dab of mayonnaise or mustard to attach the crust at the top of the sandwich (trim if needed), as shown.

2 Cut the muzzle, eyes, and insides of the ears from the remaining slice of turkey. Attach with small dots of mayo, applied with a toothpick. Cut away a small piece from the bottom of each blueberry so it sits flat, then set them in place for the nose and pupils.

3 Use a mini butterfly cookie cutter to cut shapes from the melon slices. Place them in a well of a bento box. Fill a silicone baking cup with the dressing and place in another well, along with the olives and bunny-shaped crackers. Add the sandwich to the box to complete the bento. Keep cool until ready to eat.

Olaf BENTO

PREP
5 min

COOK
15 min

SERVES
1

This **COOL HOMAGE** to Frozen's summer-loving snowman also features a nod to another character in the films—**SVEN**. The pretzels are meant to represent the **REINDEER'S ANTLERS**.

INGREDIENTS

2 (6-inch) flour tortillas

2 tablespoons cream cheese

1 slice deli ham

1 large black olive

1 rib celery

½ baby carrot

2 slices cantaloupe, cut ½-inch thick

1 slice watermelon, cut ½-inch thick

4 large pretzel twists

Special equipment
Mini flower cookie cutter

DIRECTIONS

1 Layer the tortillas, then use kitchen shears to cut them into the shape of Olaf's head, as shown. Cut the teeth from one of the scraps. Cut a slit in one of the tortilla heads with a sharp knife. Spread the other with 1 tablespoon cream cheese and layer on the ham. Sandwich with the slit tortilla.

2 Halve the olive. Use the end of a drinking straw to cut two pupils from one half. Trim two thin eyebrows from the other. Cut three thin strips of celery for Olaf's hair, as shown. Tuck the celery strips into the top of the sandwich. Roll two small balls of cream cheese and press them in place for the eyes, as shown. Add the olive pupils on top. Use more cream cheese to attach the eyebrows and a carrot nose (a toothpick works well for this task). Tuck the teeth inside Olaf's mouth and add a bit of cream cheese on top for color.

3 Use a mini flower-shaped cookie cutter to shape the melon slices. Cut out the center of each flower with a mini round cutter, then place the cut pieces in a flower with a contrasting color, as shown.

4 Break the pretzels into pieces so they resemble antlers. Place them in a bento box, along with the Olaf sandwich and melon flowers. Keep cool until ready to eat.

Mrs. Potts MELON SALAD

Turn **ORDINARY** fruit into an **EXTRAORDINARY** edible object with just a few fancy cuts. Serve it as the **CENTERPIECE** to an easygoing brunch or (you guessed it!) afternoon tea.

INGREDIENTS

1 whole cantaloupe

½ cup blueberries

1 large strawberry

1 tablespoon honey

1 cup watermelon balls

Special equipment

Melon baller

Toothpicks

TRIMMING FRUIT HOW-TO

TOOTHPICKS HOW-TO

DIRECTIONS

1 Trim 2 inches from the stem end of the cantaloupe and 1 inch from the opposite end. Halve the 2-inch piece crosswise, then cut a spout and handle from the flat portion as shown. Set all the pieces aside.

2 Scrape the seeds from the cantaloupe. Leaving the outside of the fruit intact, use a melon baller to cut the flesh and transfer to a bowl.

3 Set the empty melon atop the remaining flat melon slice. Secure it in place from the inside with toothpicks, as shown. Use more toothpicks to attach the spout, handle, and two blueberry eyes. (Break the toothpicks into shorter pieces if they are too long.)

4 Trim and reserve the top of the strawberry, then cut the remaining piece into thin slices. Trim one slice into eyebrows and a mouth, as shown. Halve the remaining slices crosswise. Use a dab of honey applied with a toothpick to attach the eyebrows and mouth to the face, and the pieces around the bottom edge of the teapot, as shown. Thread a blueberry and the strawberry top onto a toothpick, then insert it into the center of the remaining cantaloupe slice, as shown, for the pot lid.

5 Fill the cantaloupe pot with the remaining berries and cut fruit. Top with the lid. Keep chilled until ready to serve.

Alice's Teensy TEA PARTY LUNCH

White Rabbit's Petite Pocket Watch Cookies (page 27)

Little London Fogs (page 26)

This DIMINUTIVE spread of both sweet and savory delights recall some of the most MEMORABLE scenes and characters from Alice's Wonderland ADVENTURES. You can play up the theme of tiny eats by serving guests these offerings on TEACUP SAUCERS and using cocktail forks.

Dainty Queen of
Hearts Tomato Tarts
(page 26)

Wee Strawberry
Scones (page 27)

Mini Mad Hatter
Tea Sandwiches (page 26)

Dainty Queen of Hearts
TOMATO TARTS

PREP: 10 min • COOK: 30 min • MAKES: 18

INGREDIENTS

2 teaspoons olive oil

1 small leek, white and pale-green parts only, finely chopped

½ cup grape tomatoes, chopped

2 teaspoons chopped fresh basil

¼ teaspoon kosher salt

¼ teaspoon black pepper

1 refrigerated piecrust from a 15-ounce package

2 ounces goat cheese

1 egg

DIRECTIONS

1 Heat the oven to 400°F. In a small skillet over medium heat, warm the olive oil. Add the leek and cook until tender, about 5 minutes. Place in a small bowl and combine with the tomatoes, basil, salt, and pepper. Set aside.

2 Use a 2½-inch round cookie cutter to shape 18 circles from the piecrust dough, then shape 18 hearts from the remaining scraps with a mini heart cutter. When needed, gather and reroll the dough to ¼-inch thickness as you work.

3 Use a pastry tamper to mold each dough round in a well of a mini cupcake pan. Evenly divide the goat cheese among the tarts, followed by the tomato mixture. Top each tart with a dough heart.

4 In a small bowl, whisk the egg with 1 tablespoon water. Brush the tarts with the egg wash, then bake until light golden brown, about 12 minutes. Serve warm.

Little LONDON FOGS

PREP: 5 min • COOK: 10 min • SERVES: 2

INGREDIENTS

1 cup whole milk

2 sachets Earl Grey tea

4 teaspoons lavender syrup

¼ teaspoon vanilla extract

DIRECTIONS

1 In a small saucepan over medium heat, bring the milk and 1 cup of water to a simmer. Turn off the heat, add the tea bags, and steep 5 minutes.

2 Stir in the lavender and vanilla. Evenly divide between two teacups and drink immediately.

Mini Mad Hatter
TEA SANDWICHES

PREP: 5 min • COOK: 20 min • MAKES: 12

INGREDIENTS

6 ounces cream cheese, at room temperature

4 teaspoons chopped fresh dill

¼ teaspoon lemon zest

Kosher salt

Black pepper

3 Persian cucumbers

24 slices cocktail bread

DIRECTIONS

1 In a small bowl, stir together the cream cheese, dill, and lemon zest. Season with salt and pepper. Use a vegetable peeler to cut thin ribbons of cucumber. Trim the pieces to fit the cocktail bread.

2 To make each sandwich, spread a slice of cocktail bread with 1½ teaspoons of the cream cheese mixture. Layer on strips of cucumber. Trim away the crust and halve on the diagonal. Repeat with the remaining ingredients. Keep chilled until ready to serve.

White Rabbit's Petite
POCKET WATCH COOKIES

PREP: 5 min • COOK: 1 hr 15 min (includes cooling time)
MAKES: About 2½ dozen

INGREDIENTS

½ (16-ounce) roll store-bought sugar cookie dough, softened

2 tablespoons flour, plus more for dusting

1½ cups white frosting

Red food coloring

Yellow jelly beans

Chocolate sprinkles

DIRECTIONS

1 Heat the oven to 350°F and line 2 baking sheets with parchment paper. Knead together the cookie dough and flour, then roll it out to a ¼-inch thickness. Use a 2-inch round cutter to shape the dough into circles, and arrange them 2 inches apart on each baking sheet. Gather and reroll the dough as needed.

2 Place the cookies in the freezer for 10 minutes (this will help prevent too much spreading when they bake), then transfer to the oven and bake until light golden around the edges, about 12 minutes. Transfer to a rack to cool completely.

3 Place ¼ cup frosting in a small bowl and tint with red food coloring. Transfer to a piping bag fit with a small writing tip.

4 Working with one cookie at a time, use the white frosting to attach a jelly bean along the edge, as shown. Cover the center of the cookie with more frosting, and add 12 chocolate sprinkle numbers. Finish with red frosting clock hands. Repeat with the remaining cookies.

Wee
STRAWBERRY SCONES

PREP: 10 min • COOK: 40 min • MAKES: 3 dozen

INGREDIENTS

For the scones

2 cups all-purpose flour, plus more for dusting

¼ teaspoon kosher salt

2 teaspoons baking powder

¼ teaspoon baking soda

⅓ cup sugar

½ cup (1 stick) cold unsalted butter, cut into small dice

1 cup chopped strawberries

½ cup plus 2 tablespoons heavy cream

For the lemon glaze

1½ cups confectioners' sugar

¼ teaspoon lemon zest

3 tablespoons lemon juice

¼ teaspoon vanilla

DIRECTIONS

1 Heat the oven to 350°F and line a baking sheet with parchment paper. In a large bowl, stir together the flour, salt, baking powder, baking soda, and sugar. Use a pastry blender to cut in the butter.

2 Stir in the strawberries until coated, then stir in the heavy cream. Gently work the dough until it holds together (it will be slightly dry). If the dough is too dry, add more cream one tablespoon at a time.

3 Turn the dough out onto a lightly floured surface. Dust your hands with flour and gently knead a few more times. Pat it into a ½-inch-thick rectangle, use a 1½-inch round cookie cutter to shape the dough into scones, then space them 1 inch apart on the baking sheet. Freeze 15 minutes.

4 Bake the scones until they're golden brown, turning halfway through, about 20 minutes. Let cool.

5 In a small bowl, stir together all the ingredients for the glaze, then drizzle over the scones. Let the glaze set before serving.

Luigi's HOT DOG DIPPERS

PREP
10 min

COOK
1 hr 40 min
(includes rising time)

MAKES
3 dozen

In keeping with Radiator Springs resident **LUIGI'S** love for all things Italian, this version of **PIGS IN A BLANKET** replaces store-bought crescent rolls with homemade pizza dough. The result is a more savory—and some might argue **SUPERIOR**—version of a **HARD-TO-RESIST** snack.

INGREDIENTS

4 teaspoons active dry yeast

1 teaspoon granulated sugar

1¼ cups warm water (110°F)

4 cups all-purpose flour, plus more for dusting

1½ teaspoons kosher salt

¼ cup light brown sugar

1 tablespoon olive oil

12 of your favorite hot dogs

1 egg

Sesame or poppy seeds

DIRECTIONS

1 In a small bowl, stir together the yeast, granulated sugar, and water. Let sit until foamy, about 10 minutes.

2 Meanwhile, in a medium bowl, whisk together the flour, salt, and brown sugar. Make a well in the center and add the yeast mixture. With a wooden spoon, gradually combine the wet and dry ingredients into a shaggy dough. If the mixture is too wet, add a few tablespoons of flour.

3 Turn the dough out onto a lightly floured surface and knead until it's smooth and elastic, about 10 minutes. Grease a large bowl with the oil, then add the dough and turn to coat. Cover with plastic wrap and let rise in a warm spot until doubled in size, about 1 hour.

4 Heat the oven to 450°F. Line two baking sheets with parchment paper. Cut the hot dogs into 2-inch-long portions.

5 Punch down the dough and evenly divide it into 12 portions. Roll each into a 12-inch-long rope, then cut it into 4-inch lengths. Wrap each hot dog in a portion of dough and place it seam side down on a baking sheet, spacing them 2 inches apart.

6 In a small bowl, whisk the egg with 1 tablespoon water. Use a pastry brush to coat the top of each dipper with the egg wash, then sprinkle it with sesame (or poppy) seeds. Bake until the dough is golden brown, about 8 minutes. Serve immediately.

Punk Rock Pink ANIMAL PASTA

PREP
15 min

COOK
30 min

SERVES
2

The **WILDLY** vibrant hue of this noodle dish doesn't come from a bottle. It's actually the result of a **RICH SAUCE** made with fresh beets and ricotta cheese. The recipe yields enough for two, but the second serving also makes a nice leftovers lunch—**HOT OR COLD.**

INGREDIENTS

For the beet sauce

2 medium red beets, peeled and quartered

1 tablespoon olive oil

½ small yellow onion, thinly sliced

¼ teaspoon salt, plus more for seasoning

2 tablespoons ricotta cheese

Black pepper

For the pasta

2 cups cooked spaghetti

8-ounce ball fresh mozzarella

4 pitted black olives

Handful fresh Italian parsley

2 cherry tomatoes

2 slices yellow bell pepper

DIRECTIONS

1 Fill a medium saucepan with water. Add the beets and bring to a boil. Reduce the heat to low and simmer until the beets are tender, about 20 minutes. Drain and let cool.

2 Meanwhile, in a small skillet over medium heat, warm the oil. Add the onion and salt, then cook until the onions are soft and light golden, about 10 minutes.

3 Combine the beets, onions, and ricotta in a food processor. Process until smooth, about 1 minute. Season to taste with salt and pepper.

4 In a medium skillet over low heat, toss together the pasta and beet sauce. Cook, stirring constantly, until heated through. Evenly divide the pasta between two plates.

5 Cut 4 slices from the mozzarella and use the remaining cheese to make teeth. Trim a circle from the end of each olive for the pupils. To create each face, arrange parsley leaf eyebrows on each portion of pasta, as shown. Layer on mozzarella slice eyes topped with olive pupils. Set a cherry tomato nose below the eyes. Finish each face by adding a bell pepper mouth and mozzarella teeth. Serve immediately.

Aristocat-ic QUICHE MARIE

We're sure **KITTEN MARIE** would say, *"Oui, oui!"* to this savory pie—and not just because it's styled in her likeness. The filling is based on a classic French recipe called **QUICHE LORRAINE**, which features a combination of bacon, scallions, and Jarlsberg cheese. **IRRESISTIBLE** indeed!

INGREDIENTS

Cooking spray

1 store-bought refrigerated piecrust

3 scallions, chopped

5 slices cooked bacon, chopped

¾ cup shredded Jarlsberg cheese

6 large eggs

1¼ cups heavy cream

¼ teaspoon kosher salt

⅛ teaspoon black pepper

Pinch ground nutmeg

2 large black olives, halved lengthwise

¼ small red bell pepper

½ small yellow bell pepper

9 fresh chives

2 slices white cheddar

DIRECTIONS

1. Heat the oven to 350°F. Coat a 9-inch pie pan with cooking spray. Place the piecrust in the pan and crimp the edges. Scatter the scallions, bacon, and cheese in the crust and toss lightly.

2. In a medium bowl, whisk together the eggs, heavy cream, salt, pepper, and nutmeg. Pour the mixture over the other filling ingredients. Bake until the filling is set in the center and beginning to brown in some spots, about 40 minutes. Let cool slightly.

3. To make Marie's face, slice an olive half into strips for the mouth. Halve the remaining olive to form two pupils. Cut a bow and nose from the red bell pepper and two ears from the yellow bell pepper. Trim 6 chives for the whiskers and 3 for the tuft of fur. Use a round cutter to cut a circle from each slice of cheddar for the eyes. Set all the pieces in place as shown. Serve immediately.

Helpful **TIP**

For a quick, time-saving riff on this recipe, replace the bacon with diced deli ham and use your favorite pre-shredded cheese in place of the Jarlsberg.

Nemo's No Fish TACOS

Tofu takes the place of fried fish in these **ALL-VEG TACOS**. Each faux fillet is coated in panko and oven baked to achieve the same tasty texture as the **CLASSIC** version, but with **LIGHTER** results.

INGREDIENTS

1 (14-ounce) package firm tofu

1 tablespoon finely chopped garlic

3 tablespoons olive oil

¼ teaspoon kosher salt

¼ teaspoon black pepper

1 cup panko bread crumbs

½ cup shredded green cabbage

½ cup shredded purple cabbage

¼ cup shredded carrots

1 lime, halved

1 bunch cilantro, finely chopped

½ cup plain Greek yogurt

1 teaspoon ground cumin

8 (6-inch) corn tortillas, warmed

4 black olives

Special equipment
Fish-shaped cookie cutter

DIRECTIONS

1 Heat the oven to 375°F. Evenly slice the tofu into 4 square slabs. Press each with a paper towel to remove excess water. Cut the tofu with the fish-shaped cookie cutter and place in a baking dish.

2 In a medium bowl, stir together the garlic, olive oil, and ⅛ teaspoon each of the salt and pepper. Pour the mixture over the tofu, making sure to coat all sides. Marinate at room temperature for 10 minutes.

3 Place the panko crumbs in a shallow dish. Evenly coat each tofu fish with the panko by pressing it into the crumbs on all sides. Arrange the tofu fillets on a baking sheet and bake until golden, flipping halfway through, about 30 minutes.

4 While the tofu bakes, make the slaw and sauce. Cut the lime into 4 wedges. In a medium bowl, toss together both cabbages, the carrot, the juice of one lime wedge, and the cilantro, salt, and pepper. In a small bowl, stir together the yogurt, cumin, and the juice of another lime wedge.

5 To assemble each taco, arrange a bed of slaw on a tortilla, then top with one or two tofu fish and a squeeze from the remaining lime wedges. Use the end of a straw to cut eyes from the olives, then add one to each fish. Use the yogurt sauce to drizzle on stripes. Serve immediately.

Dante's BLUE CORN TACOS

Miguel's hairless, googly-eyed **DOG** is his guide and **PROTECTOR** throughout the worlds of the living and the dead. Dante's **PLAYFUL** canine face can also add a humorous twist to your regular **TACO** night.

INGREDIENTS

For the tacos

20 black olives

4 slices white cheddar

16 blue corn tortilla chips

8 blue corn taco shells

1 tablespoon canola oil

1 pound ground beef or turkey

½ cup shredded cheddar

1 cup diced tomatoes

1½ cups finely shredded red cabbage

Salsa or your favorite condiments for serving

For the seasoning mix

4 teaspoons chili powder

2 teaspoons ground cumin

1 teaspoon smoked paprika

½ teaspoon garlic powder

¾ teaspoon dried oregano

1 teaspoon salt

½ teaspoon black pepper

DIRECTIONS

1 Heat the oven to 350°F. Trim circles from the ends of 16 olives for the eyes and discard the scraps. Halve the remaining olives lengthwise for the noses. Use a mini round cutter to shape the cheese slices into 16 circles for the eyes. Trim 8 pieces from the scraps to adhere the noses. Break the tortilla chips into ear shapes, as shown.

2 Arrange the taco shells on a baking sheet. Set 2 cheddar-slice eyes and 2 olive pupils in place on each taco, as shown. Add a cheese scrap to each face and top with an olive nose. Place the shells in the oven until the cheese begins to melt, about 3 minutes.

3 In a small bowl, stir together all the ingredients for the seasoning mix. In a large skillet over medium-high heat, warm the oil. Add the ground beef or turkey and sprinkle on the seasoning mix. Cook until the meat is fully browned, about 6 minutes. Transfer to a paper towel–lined plate. To assemble each taco, fill a taco shell with ⅛ of the taco meat and top with cheddar, diced tomato, and shredded cabbage. Finish with a pair of tortilla-chip ears. Serve immediately with salsa or your favorite condiments.

Mamá Coco's
EMPANADAS

Paired with a **SALAD OR SLAW**, these **HANDHELD** meat pies make a light and tasty work lunch. Make a **BIG BATCH** and freeze them ahead of time for a real grab-and-go option you can toss right into your bag.

INGREDIENTS

1 tablespoon canola oil

1 large onion, diced

½ large red bell pepper, chopped

1 clove garlic, minced

¾ teaspoon chili powder

⅛ teaspoon cayenne pepper

4 teaspoons ground cumin

¾ teaspoon kosher salt

1 pound ground beef

2 tablespoons tomato paste

¼ cup chopped green olives

¼ to ½ cup chicken broth

15 empanada wrappers, thawed

1 egg

DIRECTIONS

1 In a large skillet over medium heat, warm the oil. Add the onion and bell pepper and cook, stirring occasionally, until softened, about 5 minutes. Add the garlic, chili powder, cayenne, cumin, and salt, and cook until fragrant, about 1 minute. Add the beef and cook, stirring occasionally, until beginning to brown, about 5 minutes.

2 Stir in the tomato paste, green olives, and ¼ cup chicken broth. Simmer, stirring occasionally, 10 minutes, to let the flavors meld. If needed, add more broth 1 tablespoon at a time as it cooks. (The mixture should be moist, but not watery.) Remove from heat and let cool.

3 Heat the oven to 400°F and line two baking sheets with parchment paper. Place an empanada wrapper on your work surface and spoon 2 tablespoons of the beef mixture onto one half. Fold the other half of the wrapper over the filling and press gently to seal. Fold in the corners of the empanada, then crimp by folding the top edge over itself. (Alternately, crimp the edge with a fork.) Place the empanada on a baking sheet and repeat with the remaining wrappers and filling, spacing them evenly on the pans.

4 In a small bowl, whisk together the egg with 1 tablespoon water. Brush the tops of the empanadas with the egg wash. Bake until golden and warmed through, about 18 minutes.

Conch Shell
MAC and CHEESE

PREP
5 min

COOK
50 min

SERVES
6 to 8

The **SECRET** to a creamy mac and cheese starts with the sauce—in this case a basic béchamel made by heating and whisking together flour, butter, and milk until rich and **VELVETY**. Blended with a trio of cheeses and an **UNEXPECTED** shell-shaped pasta, it's islands away from the boxed stuff.

INGREDIENTS

¾ pound medium pasta shells

2 teaspoons kosher salt, plus more for boiling the pasta

5 tablespoons butter, plus more for greasing the pan

5 tablespoons flour

2½ cups whole milk

2 cups shredded sharp cheddar

1 cup shredded Gruyère

⅓ cup shredded Parmesan

3 tablespoons panko bread crumbs, lightly toasted

DIRECTIONS

1 Heat the oven to 350°F. Bring a large pot of water to a boil. Season generously with salt, then add the pasta and cook until al dente, according to the package directions.

2 Grease an 8-inch baking dish with butter. In a high-sided heavy-bottom pan over medium-low heat, melt the butter. Whisk in the flour until smooth. Whisking continuously, slowly pour in the milk, a little at a time. Continue to whisk until the mixture is smooth and has thickened slightly, about 3 minutes. Remove from the heat. Stir in the salt.

3 In a large bowl, combine the pasta and roux. Stir to coat evenly. Add the cheese and blend evenly once more. Pour the mixture into the prepared baking dish. Scatter the panko over the pasta. Bake until bubbly and the topping is golden brown, about 30 minutes.

Ingredient SWAP

We prefer the flavor of sharp cheddar in our mac, but if you like more subtle flavors, you can also use mild cheddar.

Conversation Mouse COOKIES

PREP
5 min

COOK
3 hr
(includes chilling
and setting time)

MAKES
2 dozen

The **DECIDEDLY** not-mushy messages on these **VALENTINE** sugar cookies come straight from the confectioner's mouth, but you can always slip in a few of your own original musings for a **MORE PERSONAL** touch.

INGREDIENTS

For the cookies

2½ cups flour, plus more for dusting

1 teaspoon baking powder

½ teaspoon kosher salt

1 cup sugar

¾ cup (1½ sticks) unsalted butter, softened

2 eggs, room temperature

½ teaspoon vanilla extract

For decorating

1 batch royal icing (see recipe at right)

Red gel food coloring

Blue gel food coloring

Yellow gel food coloring

Red food writer

Special equipment

Mickey Mouse cookie cutter

DIRECTIONS

1 In a small bowl, whisk together the flour, baking powder, and salt. In the bowl of a stand mixer fit with a paddle attachment and set on medium-high speed, beat the sugar and butter until light and fluffy, about 3 minutes. Add the eggs and vanilla and beat to incorporate. Reduce the mixer's speed to low and blend in the flour mixture ⅓ at a time. Do not overmix.

2 Turn the dough out onto a lightly floured surface and knead a few times. Roll it into a ball and flatten into a disk. Cover with plastic, and refrigerate 30 minutes.

3 Heat the oven to 350°F. Line two baking sheets with parchment paper. Roll out the dough to ¼-inch thickness. Use the Mickey cutter to shape the dough and arrange the cookies on the baking sheets, spacing them 2 inches apart. Gather and reroll the dough as needed.

4 Bake the cookies until set and slightly crisp, turning them once halfway through, about 12 minutes. Let the cookies cool on the pans for 5 minutes, then transfer them to a rack to cool completely.

5 Evenly divide the icing among 3 bowls. Tint each with one of the gel food colorings and place in a piping bag fit with a medium writing tip. Outline the edges of each cookie, then flood the centers to cover completely, as shown. Let the icing set.

6 Use the food writer to write the desired messages on each cookie.

ROYAL ICING

INGREDIENTS

4 cups confectioners' sugar

3 teaspoons meringue powder

2 tablespoons corn syrup

DIRECTIONS

In the bowl of a stand mixer fit with the whisk attachment, combine the sugar, meringue powder, and corn syrup with 6 tablespoons warm water. Beat on medium speed until thickened but not stiff. If the icing is too thick, add another tablespoon water; if too thin, add another tablespoon sugar.

Jack's Chocolate-Topped RICE CAKES

PREP
5 min

COOK
30 min
(includes setting time)

SERVES
6

As the name suggests, these **SWEET** and salty cakes are made with just a few **SIMPLE** ingredients. The recipe easily doubles—or even triples—if your planning on **SHARING** with a large group.

INGREDIENTS

1½ cups white candy melts

2 teaspoons vegetable oil

6 plain rice cakes

⅓ cup chocolate chips

DIRECTIONS

1 Combine the candy melts and vegetable oil in a microwave-safe bowl and melt according to the package directions. Stir until smooth, then transfer to a piping bag fit with a large writing tip. Pipe a layer of candy onto each rice cake and smooth out with a spoon or offset spatula. Let the candy set.

2 Place the chocolate chips in a microwave-safe bowl and melt according to the package directions. Transfer to a piping bag fit with a small writing tip and pipe eyes and a mouth onto each rice cake, as shown. Let the chocolate set. Keep cool until ready to serve.

Ingredient SWAP

We chose white candy melts for this recipe due to their bright color, but they can be replaced with white chocolate if you prefer.

M and M MILK TOPPERS

PREP
5 min

COOK
25 min

MAKES
8

It's **TEMPTING** to cut the holes in the center of the cookies before they bake, but don't—they'll likely **SHRINK** or close altogether in the process (trust us, we've tried). If you don't own a set of **MILK BOTTLES**, you can easily find them online or at a craft store for $1 or $2 each.

INGREDIENTS

Flour, for dusting

½ (16-ounce) roll store-bought chocolate chip cookie dough

¼ cup white frosting

8 large red heart sprinkles

4 large red square or confetti sprinkles

Milk for serving

Special equipment

2- to 3-inch Mickey Mouse cookie cutter

Drinking straws

Milk bottles (optional)

DIRECTIONS

1 Heat the oven to 350°F. Line a baking sheet with parchment paper. On a lightly floured surface, roll out the dough. Use the Mickey Mouse cookie cutter to cut 8 shapes from the dough. Transfer to the baking sheet and bake according to the package directions.

2 Let the cookies cool 2 minutes, then use a drinking straw to cut a hole in the center of each one. Let cool completely.

3 Use a toothpick and frosting to attach a red sprinkle bow to four of the cookies, as shown. To serve, fill a milk bottle or small-mouth glass with milk. Set the cookie on top and thread a straw through the center opening.

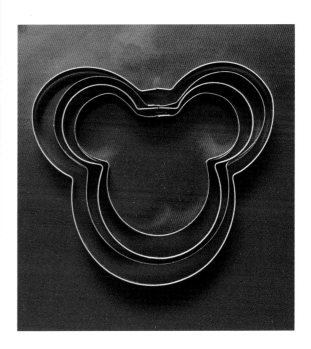

Arlo's KALE CHIPS

PREP
5 min

COOK
15 min

SERVES
4

Even if you're not a part of the **HEALTH FOOD** set, you'll be **TEMPTED** by these **DELICATE** veggie chips. To switch things up, we made our version with **DINOSAUR KALE**—a fitting variety for the recipe's **PREHISTORIC NAMESAKE.**

INGREDIENTS

1 large bunch lacinato kale, stemmed and torn into pieces

2 tablespoons olive oil

Kosher salt

DIRECTIONS

1 Heat the oven to 350°F. Use paper towels to pat dry the kale, then toss it in a large bowl with the olive oil.

2 Evenly divide the kale between two baking sheets and spread in an even layer. Bake until crisp, turning the pans halfway through, about 15 minutes. Sprinkle with salt and serve.

Helpful TIP

We like using lacinato (aka dinosaur) kale for this recipe for obvious reasons, but curly green kale is a tasty alternative. No matter which variety you choose, just be sure to keep an eye on the chips as they bake to avoid burning.